The Lost Village of
CENTRAL PARK

Hope Lourie Killcoyne

Illustrated by Mary Lee Majno

SILVER MOON PRESS
NEW YORK

First Silver Moon Press Edition 1999
Copyright © 1999 by Hope Lourie Killcoyne
Illustration copyright © 1999 by Mary Lee Majno
Edited by Barbara Leah Ellis

The publisher would like to thank Grady Turner and
Cynthia R. Copeland of the New-York Historical Society
for their help in preparing this manuscript.

For information:
Silver Moon Press
New York, NY
(800) 874–3320

Library of Congress Cataloging-in-Publication Data

Killcoyne, Hope Lourie.
The Lost Village of Central Park / Hope Lourie Killcoyne;
illustrated by Mary Lee Majno. – 1st Silver Moon Press ed.
p. cm. – (Mysteries in Time)
SUMMARY: In Seneca Village, a thriving neighborhood of African Americans
and recent immigrants in the middle of New York City in the 1850s,
friends Kayla and Sooncy face separation when the city announces
that by eminent domain it plans to take their land to build Central Park.
ISBN 1-893110-02-8
[1. New York (N.Y.) Fiction. 2. Eminent domain Fiction. 3. Land use Fiction.
4. Central Park (New York, N.Y.) Fiction. 5. Irish Americans Fiction.
6. Afro-Americans Fiction.]   I. Majno, Mary Lee, ill.   II. Title.   III. Series.
PZ7.K5562 Lo   1999
[Fic] - - dc21
99-22378
CIP

10 9 8 7 6 5 4 3 2 1
Printed in the USA

For Stephen and Lucas and Jack

TABLE OF CONTENTS

1

THE QUILTED SKY
April, 1852

SOONCY TAYLOR LOOKED INTENSELY AT THE clues hidden in the darkly colored quilt. Clever beyond her eight years and eager to prove it, she loved a good puzzle.

Unlike the quilt in her own home, this one was divided into thirds. She guessed that the zigzag pattern at the bottom was a stitched reminder that evil travels a straight path. The surest way to escape it, therefore, was to take a staggered route. The dark green section in the middle, lined throughout with blue and red stitches, was probably a map. Sooncy looked closely at the top third. The once white knots flecked about the dark blue squares had to be stars. She looked up toward the grown-ups by the stove, wanting to know if she'd guessed right, but held her tongue. Even she knew this was not a good time to interrupt—the runaways were talking. Her mother, Mr. Williams, the Reverend Smith, and another neighbor, Mr. Gable, were listening attentively.

Through the slow, thick accents, Sooncy pulled out threads of their tale: how the very quilt she now held—like others they'd left behind—was indeed laced with secret messages. At certain times, one quilt or another would be hung out over a fence near the slave cabins. Each quilt directed would-be runaways what to do. Certain patterns would alert them to pack up their belongings. Others, with specially colored arrow-like triangles, would advise which direction was safest. When the quilt with tumbling boxes appeared, it was time to escape.

Once on the dangerous path to freedom, these two, like so many before them, had followed the North Star. When travel during the day was necessary, they had looked for clumps of moss at the base of trees. Since moss grows on the shady north side, it helped keep them in the right direction.

They had jumped at the sound of dogs, jumped at the sound of white people's voices, and hidden from both. They'd been nearly eaten alive by insects and gotten sick eating the wrong berries. But at least they'd gotten here.

Mr. Williams took the lantern from the window and put it on the table. It had served its purpose, alerting runaways that this was a safe house to

enter. The two travelers in Mr. Williams's home that night were surprised to learn that he, a colored man, owned the house they were in. They looked around at the warm glow of the cartman's large living room. Where they came from, colored folks didn't even own themselves, let alone property.

There was an ebb in the adult conversation. Sooncy looked up from the quilt, thinking this was her opportunity to speak. Instead, she stared as the runaways transformed before her eyes. The taller, darker woman pulled off a black sunbonnet and a long blue skirt. Rolling down cuffed pants, then running a large hand through close-cropped hair, it became clear that she was really a *he*. Looking over at Sooncy, he laughed in a friendly, deep voice. Sooncy closed her mouth, which had fallen open. It wasn't as though she hadn't seen this kind of thing before. Runaway slaves—"running-aways" as they were called—sometimes disguised their appearance. But this particular man had made such a convincing woman that even Sooncy hadn't suspected.

She hoped for a quick recovery of pride. As the man's laughter died down she spoke up. "My daddy's helped lots of slaves escape. He smuggles them on board his ship." Mr. Williams and his neighbors exchanged glances.

The man pushed up the sleeves of his torn shirt over his muscular arms and looked at Sooncy in disbelief. "Your pappy owns a ship?" It was clear from his expression and tone that to him, northern blacks were full of surprises; they seemed to buy whatever they wanted.

Mrs. Taylor, Sooncy's mother, chuckled. "There goes that mouth again." Mrs. Taylor was a midwife and all-around nurse. She looked up from the woman runaway's bruised hand, which was caked with dried blood. "Her daddy don't own a ship. He is a sailor, though." She turned again to the bruise. A light smile came to her lips, but did nothing to brighten her eyes. She missed her husband deeply, and knew Sooncy did, too.

The woman squinted as her wound was cleaned with salt water. The tall man eased himself into a chair next to her, his weariness now flowing freely in the safety of Mr. Williams's home. "We're okay now, Betty," he said.

"I know, John. I know."

He allowed his eyes to close for a few moments.

Sooncy waited until he opened them again. Pleased that he had thought her father owned a ship, she was anxious to continue. "He stows them down below in the hold. Slips them food and water when he can." Her audience seemed to be drifting off, so she raised her voice a notch. "It's very dangerous, very important work."

Mr. Williams was back from the barrel out by his

shed with cool water for the travelers. He scolded Sooncy. "You still yapping? I should think you'd be more interested in hearing these people's fresh stories than your own stale ones. Like maybe they started as a group of three, and lost one along the way." He raised one eyebrow. "Or maybe they left the third one at home from the start because they knew that her big mouth would give them away while they were hiding."

Sooncy pursed her lips.

With her own father away more than he was home, Mr. Williams filled in when he thought a fatherly response was in order. Sooncy far preferred her father's salty cussing to Mr. Williams's sarcasm.

He turned from the sulking girl toward the weary couple. "Better yet, let them enjoy some quiet."

Mr. Gable, a neighbor who had been quietly polishing his rifle, spoke up. A nearly silent man, his dusty voice crackled. "That child always has to be the center of attention." He set his jaw at Sooncy. "It's not always where you want to be."

More unwanted fatherly advice. She came to her own defense—no one else was. "But my daddy has helped a lot of running-aways. What's the harm in saying so?"

Mr. Gable looked at her for a long moment. "Just knowing something ain't cause enough to say it." He slid his hand along the rifle's barrel. "Not by a long shot."

Reverend Smith spoke up. "Oh leave the girl be. And please put away that gun, Henry. There's no need for a weapon in here. Not now."

Mr. Gable was not a church-going man. Nevertheless he respected the minister's authority and put the gun back into its case. His fingers drifted from the hollowed-out carvings on the case to the smooth, raised scar along his cheek.

The Reverend and Mr. Williams began discussing hiding places for the running-aways. Owing to John's large size and Betty's need for further medical attention, it was agreed that he would stay in Mr. Williams's shed, she in the Taylor potato cellar. It would only be for a few days or so. Enough time to eat well, be looked after, and get some good sleep.

"It's a trying shame you have to hide up here in New York. A free state and all—but we have to be careful," Mrs. Taylor said. "That infernal Fugitive Slave Law." She broke off angrily. The law was part of the Compromise of 1850. It made it illegal to hide runaways, whether they were in a state that allowed slavery or not.

"Between slave catchers tracking down running-aways and the newspaper ads offering money for turning you all in, you poor folks just ain't safe. Not 'til you set eyes on the skies of Canada," Mr. Williams said.

John rubbed his neck and nodded sleepily. Betty, handing the empty mug back to Mr. Williams, agreed. "Amen to that."

Sooncy looked down at the quilt. She consoled herself knowing that no matter what anybody said, her daddy was doing dangerous and important work. What's more, she was, too. Her hometown of Seneca Village was a few miles north of New York City. The village didn't get many running-aways. It wasn't a regular stop on the Underground Railroad. But that just made it all the more exciting when these weary "friends" came through. Harboring slaves might have been against man's law, but not doing so, she felt, was against God's.

She picked up the tattered, intricate quilt and put it on Betty's lap. The woman had fallen asleep right there in the chair. Her good hand positioned itself instinctively around a well-worn corner of the quilt flecked with little white bumps. Sooncy watched the woman's thumb caress one of the gray knots. It was the knot of the North Star.

2

PLACE OF THE STONE

IT WAS MOVING DAY, MAY 1, 1852, THE MOST hectic day of the year. New York City leases ended on May 1, so many renters moved that day in hopes of finding better lodgings. Out of their old apartments by nine in the morning and into new ones by noon, the city became a frenzied jumble of people, their possessions, and the cartmen who moved them. It was a turbulent and unsettling time for renters. But it was the best day of the year for cartmen. On this day, white people fought each other off for Andrew Williams's services. Some even called him *sir*.

Now, at two o'clock, the dust and dried horse manure had settled. Mr. Williams let his horse, Angel, rest a while. Sitting atop his cart smoking a long clay pipe—just as all the white carters did—

his attention came to rest on a forlorn trio across the street and down a few buildings.

He took a long draw on his pipe. The woman, he could see, was long-suffering, used to hard work and hardship. She'd probably get a job cooking or cleaning or some such for a rich family, a job that used to be done by colored women until all the potatoes in Ireland rotted and all the people there ran to America.

The ailing man, skinny as a corn stalk, didn't have long for the world.

But the young girl was hard to look away from. She couldn't be more than seven. So terribly thin, it looked like you could take her across your knee and snap her in two like kindling. Now as a rule, Andrew Williams didn't spend his time thinking about poor white kids; he had enough to think about looking after his own kind. But there was something about this one. Something special.

As struck as he was with the girl, it bothered him later on that he hadn't taken longer to look in the mother's eyes. Looking into someone's eyes was the surest way to get a sense of a person. Mr. Williams was known far and wide for his ability to size up people quickly. In the time it took to say hello and hear it back he might have seen something, avoided an unnecessary risk. Well. Can't think of everything. Mostly what he did think about right then was that he had a perfectly good rental property sitting empty. And these people obviously needed a place to live.

He approached them, tipping his hat. He told them about the little village a short ways north of the city, and the availability of a small but decent home there. "Big enough for three," he said, thinking to himself that they'd most likely be down to two, soon. "Called Seneca Village. Folks say Seneca's Indian for 'place of the stone.' It's rocky land, all right. Got your work cut out for you if you're going to plant anything."

Mrs. McBean cleared her throat and spoke. "We're used to rocks, it's all we had back in Ireland." She squinted up at Mr. Williams, shielding her eyes from the sun. "I'd like a nice bit of land again, plant a few herbs for my cures and such, but I wouldn't live off it. I'll never put my faith in the land again." She looked down at her husband, who was sitting on the ground resting with his head between his knees. Her thoughts flicked back to an earlier time in Ireland. She could still see him with a hoe thrown over one broad shoulder, their daughter tossed up on the other. It was hard to believe that was less than a year ago.

Kayla got up from beside her father and pulled on her mother's blouse. She didn't want this man to leave without them. She had been glad to leave the damp gloom of the cellar. Used to a life of farming, Kayla viewed the apartment as unnatural. It was like living buried in the ground beneath an upright box. But leaving that apartment was like leaving Ireland all over again. Once more, the terrifying whole of America stretched out before them. This man was a godsend. Offering a specific destination—north to a village away from the bustle of the city—sounded like heaven. After a short, whispered discussion with her mother, Kayla spoke. "You must have been sent by an angel, sir," she said softly.

Andrew Williams laughed. "I don't know if an angel sent me, but one sure enough brought me. This here is Angel," he said, patting his horse, "and I'm Andrew Williams."

Kayla stroked Angel's cheek and returned Mr. Williams's smile.

After the rest of the introductions were made, Kayla and her mother helped Mr. McBean to his feet, and up into the wooden cart.

As a tired Angel plodded up Broadway, the buildings thinned out. There were a few homes north of Fourteenth Street, but most people lived well below it. Several miles north of the city, they passed what Kayla would later learn were bone-boiling plants and soap-making plants. There were also several slaughterhouses. As used to the raw elements of a hard life as she was, the smell was dreadful even for

her. She pinched her nose tight. Mrs. McBean, near sick at the smell herself, nevertheless put Kayla's hand back in her lap. Good or bad, life was to be endured. She wouldn't have any daughter of hers putting on airs, or trying to keep bad ones out.

Mr. Williams pulled on Angel's reins to slow her up a bit as they neared the huge boulder, Nanny Goat Hill. As they cleared it, they turned right. Kayla took in the view. What first stood out was the huge reservoir. It was wide and tall, and built of stone. In the valley between the reservoir and her lay a quaint village. She liked the look of it at once. The tidy homes laid out before the reservoir looked like dollhouses arranged neatly in front of a large toy chest. Kayla was grateful the houses didn't look like the rickety shacks they'd just passed near the foul-smelling factories. These houses weren't wobbling on rocks. They weren't bunched here and scattered about there like jacks tossed in the dirt. This place had streets, gardens, and churches. This place had pride.

Mrs. McBean looked past the buildings to the villagers. Although many of the residents out and about that day were white—Irish immigrants and others—all Mrs. McBean saw was a sea of black faces. She looked down at her husband. Weary and quite ill, he had slept with his head in her lap the whole trip. *Mother of God*, Mrs. McBean thought to herself. *Where have we landed now?*

3

JUNE 1855

THREE YEARS PASSED SINCE THE McBEANS HAD settled in Seneca Village. Enough time for Kayla's father to die, for her mother to give birth to a still-born baby, and for Kayla and her mother to find work as day servants cooking and cleaning for the Ellertons. Just as Mr. Williams had predicted, their employers were a well-to-do family over in nearby Bloomingdale. Bloomingdale was a wealthy suburb north of West Eightieth Street.

But three years was not enough time for Kayla, now ten, to get over her pleasure at their little home. She spent whatever time she could looking out their windows. Two windows! One to catch the sun and one to watch it go. The little thatched shack in Ireland hadn't had any.

Her favorite treasure was her hand-made bed.

Mr. McBean built it for her just before his death. Roughly made though it was, it was important to them both. She had never had a bed all to herself. Back in County Clare, she had shared a bed with her ailing uncle. Down in the gloomy city cellar, all three McBeans had shared one dirty, rag-filled pallet on the floor. This bed was like a message from her father, a message of permanence—she finally had a real home.

Beyond that special item, Kayla was grateful for all she had. Sometimes she would even deprive herself of certain things for a time just so that she could then appreciate them all the more. She would wait until after she was almost faint with hunger to eat, or until the cool night air had chilled her to pull her warm woolen blanket up to her neck.

The only thing the house and the village had not yet offered her, though, was a friend. Once she had one, she promised herself, she'd keep her forever.

For Mrs. McBean, three years seemed not enough time for her to stop asking herself why they had come this far to live in a town of coloreds. In response, she'd hear her late husband's voice— that rich Irish voice—scolding her for not appreciating the good that had come her way: *Stop your moanin' Sheila. You've a small patch of land in which to grow your roots and an ample potato cellar to store them and keep them cool. You've steady work, and most of all, a lovely daughter by your side, wise and kind-hearted.* Mrs. McBean would nod and smile, a quiet "Aye" escaping her lips. Kayla knew at these times that her mother was hearing her father. She heard him, too. *I know you're grateful for what you have little Kaylie. Just remember to use it to its best advantage. America is full of opportunity.*

IT WAS FRIDAY, TEA TIME AT the Ellerton home. China cups clinked gently against china saucers. The aroma of coffee, fresh baked goods, and flowery perfume mingled in the gleaming front parlor. One woman's voice darted in and around it all.

"Oh, my, yes. Mr. Ellerton is noble—at times too noble!"

Mrs. Ellerton chattily held court with several friends who had come for luncheon. Mrs. McBean silently held a sterling silver tray with cookies and pastries she had baked.

"You know," continued Mrs. Ellerton at no one's prompting, "I don't think that even I know all the charitable institutions in which my dear husband is involved. Funding libraries here, looking for park space there . . . " She sighed.

"You know," she whispered loudly, flitting to her next favorite topic, "people say it's quite insane of me with this large house to get by with so little live-in help. My best cook refuses to live in." Mrs.

Ellerton glared in the direction of Kayla's mother.

Sheila McBean reddened slightly and turned to adjust the drapes. Kayla came in with a fresh pot of coffee and a trivet. She placed them on the table before Mrs. Ellerton. "But the two I have do seem to get more done in a day than even I had thought possible. And I must admit the cooking is exceptional." She waved a forkful of seedcake for emphasis. "The woman won't let the child go to school—you know the Irish—they think the public schools are anti-Catholic, of all things. So I let her bring the girl along. It's the least I can do." She nodded in agreement with herself and ate her cake.

Kayla stole a look at her mother, who still had her back to the gathering. Mrs. McBean was as rigid as a rolling pin. Kayla bristled at the way Mrs. Ellerton spoke of her and her mother right in front of them, as if they weren't even there. She wished she had the courage to stop this foolish talk, but that wasn't her way. She sighed, wishing it were.

"Well, Elizabeth," one of the older ladies said, "you are quite lucky that your girls seem neither flighty nor irresponsible." There was a general murmuring of agreement.

"True, but I do sometimes wonder about her judgment. You know where they live, of course." She waved a limp hand in the general direction of Seneca Village. "Coloreds and whites living right next to each other. Farm animals wandering all about."

The ladies murmured and clucked their tongues. A younger woman dressed completely in pink spoke up. "All those shanties! Quite a blight. I read recently that fully half the people who live in our city now are foreigners." The ladies nodded. She went on, "Really now, there are more immigrants and more tumbledown shacks every time one turns around. Rather like earthworms and mushrooms after a rainstorm!"

Light laughter filled the room. Proud and pleased with herself, the young woman blushed freely, completing her pink ensemble.

Mrs. McBean grew silently defensive. Seneca Village was not full of shanties. These women had assuredly never been there. She disliked hearing others—especially ignorant others—speak ill of Seneca. It was like having Kayla scolded in front of her. She knew what was lacking in both, but didn't need to hear anyone else's opinion on the matter.

Waiting silently for further instructions from Mrs. Ellerton, Kayla dusted the frame of Robert James's portrait. Dear, sweet RJ. She looked up into the gray-blue eyes of Mrs. Ellerton's only child. Her heart fluttered a bit. The artist had ably caught the thirteen-year-old's dark good looks, leaving out his frail sickliness. She hoped his health would improve soon. He was her only friend.

Tomorrow was Saturday, her "day off" by herself. Her mother's only day off was Sunday. But Saturdays were Kayla's alone. Those were her days to do the McBean washing, mending, and cooking. She'd also wash and mend for some of the neighbors now and then. Most especially for two local bachelors. There was Officer Hale, the policeman who lived down the lane, and Mr. Gable, a day laborer who lived a few blocks north.

Kayla turned back toward the carefree chatter of the women. She felt years older than ten.

AT COLORED SCHOOL #3, ONE of several New York schools for colored children, Catherine Thompson, the teacher, looked up from the papers she was grading. She sat back, and smiled. Sooncy Taylor, today's student teacher, was at the front of the class. It was the eleven-year-old's favorite place to be. The school used the Lancaster Method of teaching, where older students were called on to teach and monitor the younger ones. Recitation was a key element of the method, although Sooncy tended to stray from the lesson plans.

Miss Thompson and the children listened as Sooncy talked, or rather performed.

"All you who come to AME Zion know what Reverend Smith calls our village." Colored School #3 was the only school in Seneca Village. And

21

although the school was in the basement of the African Union Church, most villagers attended the African Methodist Episcopal Zion Church, "AME Zion" for short. Sooncy looked around and called on the raised hand of Elia, Andrew Williams's seven-year-old grandson. "Stand please, Elia."

The child spoke, lisping through four spaces left by newly departed baby teeth: "He says, 'God smiles on Seneca Village. We are the lantern in the window of his house.'"

Sooncy smiled. "Good, Elia. You may 'thit' down, now." The class giggled. Sooncy walked back and forth in front of the classroom in the dramatic style that the Reverend sometimes used. Miss Thompson shook her head and smiled.

"We are living in a very special place, children," Sooncy said. "Most of us colored folks own our own homes. Our daddies have the vote. We have so much opportunity—to help ourselves, to help each other, to help friends we don't yet know." She stopped walking back and forth and looked directly at the little faces watching her every move. "You know what I'm talking about."

Miss Thompson cleared her throat and rose from her chair in the back. The children turned their heads to look. "That's enough preaching for today, Miss Taylor. It's time to get back to our lesson plan and back to earth. We'll all be a lot more able to help ourselves and others if we can read and write, wouldn't you agree?"

The class spoke in unison, Sooncy among them. "Yes, Miss Thompson."

Sooncy retook her place at the end of a bench as Miss Thompson led the class in recitation. Sooncy's lovely voice sang along with the singsong poems, but her mind drifted out the window, to the girl in her root cellar.

AT A FLEABAG HOTEL DOWN IN the city, not far from where the McBeans had once lived, two rough-looking men were in the process of going over the descriptions of the runaway slaves they were looking for. The heavier man drawled: "And these two: Man, light complected, five foot ten or so, lashes across the top of his back. Name of Thomas. 'Bout forty years old. Girl, name of Sarah. Looks like him, tall, no scars, but has a limp."

The thin man whined. "I've heard this a million times already. Let's go get a drink. Tomorrow's the day we start a-hunting; let's enjoy tonight while we can. See what pleasures this city has to offer two Southern gentlemen such as ourselves."

The heavy one stood up and looked out the window at the bustle of activity on the street below. "We only have a week. One week from Sunday, we go. 'Cause come hell or high water, I'm starting my new life on time." His voice lowered, as he spoke more to himself than his partner. "I'm perfect for that job . . . a natural born overseer. It's high time Mr. Villum noticed it. I'll be the best darned whip-cracker he ever had. Be a lot easier looking after slaves in the field than tracking them down all over this godforsaken place." He turned to his partner. "But I want to go home rich. Don't you?"

The other one rubbed his bristly chin and nodded.

"All right then," he continued, leaning his back-side against the window. "We'll hit the nightspots, but don't get blind drunk again. We might learn something useful tonight if we keep our wits about us, and be able to use it tomorrow."

4

MEETING AT THE SPRING

IT WAS A GOOD DAY FOR WASHING. THERE WAS A strong sun to dry the clothes. Earlier that morning, before dawn, Kayla had picked up Officer Hale's wash to do along with her own. Doing his wash and mending every Saturday was a good way to earn more money.

Kayla suspected Mr. Hale was sweet on her mother. He sometimes delayed picking up his laundry until Sunday afternoon when he knew Sheila McBean would be there.

Kayla liked him, though. He had a good heart. He held prayer meetings with coloreds and whites in his home, meetings she and her mother had been invited to attend many times. He was always turned down, politely. The McBeans had gone once to All Angels, the mixed-race church on Eighty-fifth Street.

It was one of three such churches in town. After that service, Mrs. McBean told Kayla that they would spend Sundays alone together. "God will understand. We're Catholics. They aren't." Kayla understood, too, but she wanted to go as much for meeting people as anything else. After three years in Seneca Village, she still didn't feel like she belonged.

As she pinned wet clothes to the line, Kayla remembered today was the day she was also to do Mr. Gable's wash. It meant boiling, beating, and ringing out more clothes, but it also meant more money. Some stray dogs wandered by. She hoped they wouldn't soil the clean laundry.

Mr. Gable was lean and wiry, his handsome face marked by a long welt across his left cheek. He kept to himself, never saying more than he had to, but in his own quiet way he made Kayla feel that he appreciated her. Kayla's mother said he just liked her because she was a white girl doing a colored man's wash. Kayla tried not to pay attention to her mother when she went on about Mr. Gable. He didn't put on any airs at all, unlike Mrs. Ellerton.

Kayla cut her way through people's yards as she did now and again to get to his place on Eighty-sixth Street. She noticed large amounts of laundry hanging in the yard between AME Zion Church and Andrew Williams's home. It wasn't the first time she had seen those clotheslines filled end to end.

Whenever there was this much laundry there was also extra food being brought into the church. And people whom she didn't know would be walking around. They were always colored people. They had a slow way of talking, and a fearful, nervous way of looking around.

Mr. Gable was in his yard, working in the garden. He looked up and nodded at Kayla, a pleasant smile on his lips. She smiled back, picked up the bundle from his back porch, and headed home. Pausing a moment, she caught sight of Mr. Williams hitching up Angel to the cart. She waved shyly. Mr. Williams nodded and smiled back at her.

"Morning, young lady," he called out cheerfully.

Her smile broadened. "Morning!" As she turned away, something on a clothesline caught her eye. Among the pants and shirts, between some scarves and skirts, Kayla noticed a quilt. It was catching the cool, gentle breeze from the north. She'd seen ones similar to it before. But aside from the one that occasionally hung out Mr. Williams's window, she never saw the same two twice. This one was particularly beautiful. She wanted to stop and look at it more closely, but she had work to do. She shooed away a pig and goat that were sniffing at her, and walked home.

Down at the spring getting more water for the extra washing, Kayla saw Sooncy Taylor. She put down her buckets and waited her turn.

Over the years she'd seen Sooncy many times. You couldn't help but notice her. Tall and beautiful; she had a commanding presence. Her broad smile could light up an entire room. Not that she'd ever smiled at Kayla. Most times Kayla saw Sooncy, she usually had a bunch of little kids around her, vying for her attention.

It was Sooncy and her mother who got Kayla's mother through the stillborn birth. Kayla remembered Mrs. Taylor's soothing and reassuring way. Mrs. McBean had been fortunate to have such a good midwife. Kayla had hoped they all might get to be friends. They hadn't. Though they lived in the same small village, they occupied two different worlds. Kayla lived down closer to the spring in the shabbier part of town. It was still respectable, but not as fancy as where the Taylors, the Williamses, and Mr. Gable lived. Everyone on that street had two-and three-story homes, some with big wraparound porches.

Kayla also knew that Sooncy went to school. That, to Kayla, was the greatest of her riches.

Sooncy was aware of Kayla watching her from behind. When the McBeans had first come to Seneca, Sooncy was suspicious of them. Her own family on her mother's side had been in the village since its earliest days in the 1820s, when it was all farmland

and the colored folks had settled it. Mr. Williams, an old family friend, had bought the first lots.

Sooncy's father's people came in the 1830s. They had moved over from York Hill when the city took over that land to build the reservoir. The families in York Hill had all been paid by the city to leave, but her father told her how upsetting it was to be ordered from your home, then see it torn down by strangers.

With Ireland's famine in the 1840s, more and more immigrants had found their way uptown to the little village. Seneca had always had a few whites. There were the native-borns and German immigrants, too, but the older folks talked about how the Irish were different. Set themselves up against the blacks. Took their jobs away—waiting tables, cleaning houses—then got all angry when talk turned to ending slavery. Actually, it was more the Irish down in New York City you had to watch out for. The ones that came up to Seneca were all right, as far as it goes. Sooncy felt that the McBeans fit in okay—they didn't make waves. The father died, and the mother probably would have, too, if her own mother hadn't stayed with her the night she lost the baby. Sooncy helped, too. Anyhow, Sooncy had to admit that at least they had never interfered with the secret work of the village. They hadn't helped—but then again, they hadn't been asked to.

Sooncy thought about the day ahead. Do the

wash. Hang the wash. Run an errand for Mrs. Ryan. Go to the river for kindling, then head home to see if her mother needed help. Mrs. Taylor was hiding a running-away named Sarah. Sarah's father, Tom, was with Mr. Williams. Or, in the secret language of the underground, the Taylors had one load of "dry goods," the Williamses one load of "hardware." The two were due to leave in a week. Sarah needed that time to rest. Mrs. Taylor was tending to her lame knee, saying it wasn't ready for the journey north just yet.

AT THE SPRING, SOONCY FILLED her buckets. Kayla waited. Sooncy turned around and looked at the pale, freckled girl. And in the morning stillness where the two found themselves alone, they smiled at one another.

Kayla worked up her courage and spoke first. "Good morning."

Sooncy laughed. "You can talk!" It hit her then that Kayla wasn't such a bad sort. What's more, Sooncy wanted company. Running it over in her mind briefly, she invited Kayla to go on the errands with her.

Kayla thought a moment. She knew that her mother would disapprove. Except for rare trips downtown and working for the Ellertons in Bloomingdale, Kayla did not leave the village. Mrs.

McBean had scared her plenty with her stories. There were lunatics who might escape from the many asylums in the area and do heaven knows what to a young girl. Bad men who hunted down runaway slaves lurked behind trees. She wasn't colored, true, but did she really want to be in the woods with people like that, her mother would ask. Plus there were just plain ordinary folk blind with drink—you never knew what they might do to anyone.

Still, it sounded like fun. It was different. She wanted company, too. *My work can wait*, she thought. *My mother will never find out.*

They agreed to meet up after they had hung out their washing.

5

BLACKBIRDERS

THEIR FIRST STOP WAS MRS. RYAN, WHO LIVED just south of the spring. Seneca Village was laid out along streets, but the area to the north, south, and east was all rocks and boulders. There were streams and swamps and hills. Shanties were scattered about. Garbage was strewn everywhere. Dead animals rotted where they fell.

Below a stream they came upon the small house, so poorly made that it looked as though it might have been built in the dark. Rubbish littered the yard, and goats butted each other to get at it. The place smelled.

"Looks like an ordinary house, right?" Sooncy said.

"I guess."

"It's really a drinking house, a place where people

go to drink whiskey all night long. Mrs. Ryan runs it."

"How do you know?"

"I work for her now and again. Delivering messages. She pays well. And," Sooncy added proudly, "I'm the only girl she uses. Mostly it's boys that get all the good messenger jobs. But I can write and a lot of them can't. Mrs. Ryan just tells me the message and I write it down for her. Then I go to the grocer or chemist or to her son's over at the shore or wherever. Let's go in."

Sooncy knocked on the door. A small, impish looking woman opened it a crack. Though nearly noon, she looked as if she had just awakened. Her eyelids squinted against the bright sun.

"That you, Sooncy?"

"Yes, ma'am."

"I knew you were smart, but not smart enough to read my mind. I was just now thinking I had a message that needed running. Come on in and I'll fetch you a scrap of paper."

Kayla did not want to go in, but the idea of waiting outside alone was even less appealing. She followed meekly.

Earthen jugs of alcohol lined the far wall. A mismatched group of wooden chairs stood guard in front of the jugs. An unmade bed was against the wall under a window. The floor was of beaten dirt. Even Kayla, used to all kinds of living conditions, couldn't imagine sleeping in this room.

Mrs. Ryan, who had been muttering to herself, turned around with paper and pencil in her hands. It was then she noticed Kayla. "You've brought a helper, have you? Well, I'll not be doubling your pay, but I think I might find some candy about. What's your name then, lass?"

"Kayla."

"Ah, Sooncy, my girl. You're taking up with the right sort of folk now." She looked at Kayla again. "Is it right off the boat you are?"

"No, ma'am. We came from County Clare several years ago."

Mrs. Ryan, being from another part of Ireland, lost interest and got back to her own affairs. "Now, Sooncy, I want you to go down to Piggery Row and tell Mr. Reinhold that I'll not have his young son coming 'round here anymore. The boy's barely twelve, and that's too young to be drinking up my whiskey." Sooncy wrote quickly. "Now if you'll pardon me, I'll give you your candy, your dime, and send you on your way."

FIFTY-NINTH STREET HAD BEEN given the fitting name of Piggery Row. Mr. Reinhold's business was close to Eighth Avenue, wedged between two large rock outcroppings. Before the girls could even see the slaughterhouse they smelled it. The sounds were the stuff of nightmares—final screams from doomed animals. Around the main building, animal innards were flung here and there. Strewn about, too, were heads of cows, pigs, and horses. Blood ran in sinister streams. It flowed from gutter pipes over the rocky ground and into the sticky earth.

Behind an empty pigsty, several barefoot boys were playing marbles. They shot the smooth glass balls into a shallow hole called a "pot." It occurred to Kayla then and there that she wasn't so much aware of the differences between coloreds and whites as the differences between boys and girls. Boys never helped with cooking or cleaning or hanging out clothes to dry. If a boy were holding a clothesline, he was far more likely to be using it to lasso a pig than hang the family wash.

She wondered which one was the Reinhold boy. The thought of meeting the father who allowed him to go out drinking was unsettling.

Mr. Reinhold was a hearty, beefy man. He smiled broadly at Sooncy, wiping his large hands on a darkly stained apron. Sooncy, knowing the butcher couldn't read, saved him any embarrassment by repeating Mrs. Ryan's message from memory. Kayla could tell from the changing look on his ruddy face that he disapproved of his son's idle ways. She could also tell that he would deal with his son severely.

As the girls passed the boys on their way out,

Mr. Reinhold made a beeline for a stocky blond boy. His friends scattered like a group of marbles hit dead-on.

Heading back north to the river for firewood, the girls ran across Seneca Villagers and others. Several of them recognized Sooncy and waved. Dragging sacks behind them, they were carrying on the Saturday business of redeeming what they had found—some called it "scavenged"—throughout the week. Bones went to the bone-boiling factories: Mr. Menck's at West Sixty-sixth Street, or Mr. Moller's at West Seventy-fifth. Rags went to manufacturers of paper or shoddy, the cheap cloth folks used to make homespun clothes. Bottles, cans, paper—just about anything that could have a second life meant money in return.

The girls reached the river and watched the passing ships. A few other people dotted the coastline just north of them. Some were gathering wood like themselves, some were fishing.

Sooncy, natural instructor that she was, decided to go to work. She held up a stick. "Recitation is the key to success in the Lancastrian Method. I will now teach you the best sea chantey I know. The men on my father's ship made it up just for him." Mr. Taylor had been a sailor for years—ever since he lost his job as a waiter to an Irish immigrant.

"Listen to me first, then we'll do it together."

"Okay."

"Before we begin, there are a few words you might not know. First, a flapjack's what you call a pancake."

"I know that!" Kayla protested.

"Okay, smarty pants, what's a blackjack?"

Kayla shrugged. "Oh, wait. I know. It's a man who catches runaway slaves."

"Heck no, that's a blackbirder. A blackjack is what they call a colored man at sea, a black sailor. Got it?"

Kayla nodded.

"Okay, here we go. It's supposed to sound like 'Oh! Susanna.'"

Oh, the flapjacks from this blackjack
are the best we've ever found.
And we're glad that Sailor Taylor's
out at sea and not on ground.

So we sing this little chantey
for the big man from the shanty,
that sweet little Seneca shanty,
in the wilds of old New York.
Sailor Taylor, oh won't you fry for me?
Won't you go below with a "yo ho ho"
and fry some cod for me?

Kayla clapped. "Sooncy, that's wonderful! But you don't live in a shanty. Your house is beautiful."

"I know. They were just going for the rhyme. Okay, let's do it together."

After a bit of coaching, the two girls sang together in harmony. The sound of their mingling voices was pleasing to them both. They were glad they had this part of the river to themselves.

At least they thought they had it to themselves. Two nearby voices, men's voices, began singing Mr. Taylor's song.

"No wait," one said. "Here. Listen. 'Sailor Taylor, oh, don't you cry for me, 'cause I'm going to string your daughter from this here old apple tree.'"

Stepping out from behind some bushes, two ragged-looking men could barely contain their laughter. They were blackbirders, "human blood-hounds" in search of runaway slaves.

"Don't make a move," the heavy one commanded hoarsely. His large hand dug into Sooncy's shoulder.

The girls froze in terror.

6

DANGER BY THE RIVER

WILLARD SLAPPED THE THIGH OF HIS MUD-stained pants.

"Edmund, I think we done struck gold—black gold." With a flourish, he recited the description of Sarah, the missing slave girl.

Edmund protested. "But this one ain't lame, Willard."

Willard snorted and picked up a large stick out of the girls' pile of kindling. He sliced the air with it. "I can fix that," he said. "Anyhow. She's close enough. Better than close enough. Right, Sarah?"

He winked at her, then peeled the bark off the stick as if grooming it for use. Sooncy stared at the ground sightlessly. "Actually, we're doing Villum a favor. Don't you think he'd rather have her than someone can't even walk right? Anyhow, who's here to stop us?" He continued working on the stick.

The thick silence was broken by Kayla's thin voice. "I am," she said. The two men exploded into laughter. Undaunted, Kayla continued, mustering all the courage she could. "My father will stop you. I'm not kidding. This girl does our wash, cleans our house. You take her, he'll kill you." Again they laughed, but not as heartily.

"What's some Paddy drunk going to do to us?" Edmund said, puffing out his chest like a scrawny rooster.

His words enraged Kayla. "My father is no Paddy drunk. He's an officer of the law, a Municipal Police Officer. Today's his day off, and he's coming here any minute to go fishing and help us haul back the firewood."

Sooncy stole a look at Kayla. The men looked at each other uncertainly. Had Kayla stopped them?

Willard spat out his words. "You tell them negrahs we're coming to get them. Y'hear?"

"I don't know who you're talking about," Kayla retorted.

He ignored her. "And tell your daddy he'd be a fool to protect them, and a lawbreaker. They'll lock him up for messing with our business transaction. It's agin' the law for anyone to mess with a slave catcher's duty, especially an officer." He cracked the stick over his knee. Both girls flinched. "You two

have just made some dangerous enemies for your-selves. You better hope we don't see you again." He spat disgustedly into the woodpile and turned away. Edmund gave them both one last, long look. Then he followed his partner.

"Willard," Edmund panted, struggling to keep up, "Why'd we let 'em go?"

Willard slowed his pace slightly. "I don't buy that story for a minute. But we learned something very valuable just now."

"We did?"

"I'll bet my pistol those two live in that inter-mixed shantytown we heard about last night."

Edmund rubbed his eyes. The drink had gone to his head quickly the night before, and he only dimly remembered hearing talk of some small village, Senator or Seneca—something like that. "Yeah, but I don't get it. If we don't follow 'em now, who knows how long those others'll be there? Mr. Villum's gonna kill us. Or worse. You know how spiteful he is. Got more venom in him than a rattler."

Willard stopped to face his partner. "Edmund, this will probably be our only chance to ever see New York City. We got us a full week here." He slowed the pace of his talking to a condescending crawl. "Let's say they are there now. You want to haul them people around—chain them to our beds for a week? I want my fill of this place before I head back to civilized society. And I aim to be mighty uncivilized here," he said with a wink.

"But Willard," Edmund whined, "If we wait, we'll miss them. I just know it."

"Don't you worry. Them other two might go, but they're small change, anyhow." He smiled broadly. "Our real pot of gold will still be setting there. We'll carry out Mr. Villum's revenge yet. That you can rely on." He put his arm around Edmund and started walking again. "Right now we're going back to the city. We'll let things cool off up here. Give it a week and they'll think everything's blown over. Trust me."

IT WAS SEVERAL MINUTES AFTER the sound of the men's footsteps had died away before the two girls looked at each other. Kayla couldn't believe it—couldn't believe that her words had such a powerful effect on those two awful men.

Sooncy, too, was full of emotion: anger. She faced Kayla. "Don't you never do that again. I'll take care of myself. I don't need no ignorant little Paddy like you."

Kayla was speechless. She hadn't expected gratitude—her still-frightened mind hadn't even gotten that far—but she certainly didn't expect this.

In silence, Sooncy gathered a sheet of kindling, and dragged it back to Seneca Village. Kayla followed a good distance behind.

That night, after her mother had fallen asleep, Kayla was still greatly troubled by the day's events. She got up and looked out the window. She saw a few dark figures moving in the darker night. The last one looked kind of like Sooncy. But this girl had a limp.

7

DANGER NEXT DOOR

ANDREW WILLIAMS AND HIS WIFE SAT IN THEIR usual pew, two benches back from the pulpit, dead center. Their family flanked them, Elia sitting next to his grandfather. The benches were hard and narrow. The newly built church wasn't as big as All Angels or the African Union, but it had by far the biggest congregation.

Reverend Smith waited silently until he had everyone's attention. Parents shushed their children, grandfathers cleared their throats, and elderly aunts fanned themselves. Mrs. Taylor swatted away a horsefly. As the last giggle ended and the focus shifted to the front, the Reverend looked up from the pulpit. "God is testing us this week. The Fugitive Slave Law is as evil as we knew it would be."

Some women clucked sympathetically, tentatively.

Several men nodded. They didn't yet know where the sermon was headed, but they knew all too well the negative impact of the five-year-old law.

"The Compromise of 1850 was a compromise with the devil."

More, louder agreement rose from the pews.

"The devil is a long way down. You make a deal with him, meet him halfway, you're still in a deep pit." He paused. "That's a long way from heaven." More nods, more affirmations. "But we in Seneca Village are blessed. We trick the devil every day."

The congregation laughed.

"We are thankful to have been of service to our new friends." He nodded at the Taylors and the Williamses, in whose homes Sarah and her father were currently hiding. "But danger is growing. Yesterday afternoon, down at the North River, young Miss Taylor had her life threatened by a couple of the devil's own—bounty hunters out to take our friends and put them back into bondage."

The parishioners gasped. He waited as this news sank in.

Sooncy looked down into her lap. He continued. "We've faced this kind of thing before. But let me remind you, it isn't just villainous types we've had to worry about. There have been well-meaning, misguided whites who have felt compelled to obey the Fugitive Slave Law." The congregation snorted in

derision. "These folks have turned running-aways over to the authorities. But this, this is the first time one of our own has been threatened." Soncy looked deeper into her lap, uncomfortable with the stares of those around her.

Poor child, they whispered softly. She bit her lip and lifted her head. She looked past them, straight ahead at the Reverend. He continued. "It is *chilling*, yes. But we can't let it *freeze* us—can't let any of this keep us from protecting *all* our brothers and sisters."

Soncy listened, but her ears started humming. Her thoughts were growing louder than the Reverend's voice. She had not told the whole story yesterday. She hadn't told her mother what had really happened at the river. She hadn't told her that Kayla had been there, too. Kayla's words, however much they had saved her, were humiliating. And when Mrs. Taylor brought her daughter over to Mr. Williams's that night so that he could hear first-hand, Soncy hadn't told him either. She was too embarrassed, too angry. At that point, she couldn't go back on her story. *Why didn't I tell them Kayla was with me? Why didn't I tell them?* The Reverend Smith's words broke through again.

"We'll have to count on neighbors we haven't gone to before. There's no sin in asking for help. But there could be great danger in choosing unwisely. It is God's will to help those we can. And we do, with honor and pride. It is his pleasure that we accept help when we need it, as well. The wise person knows when to give help as well as when to take it." The Reverend looked at Sooncy. "He wants us all to work together, to fit together. That's what community is about. That is most especially, what this one is about." He picked up his Bible and hymnal as "Amens" were heard from the nodding crowd.

"All right then." He looked toward Andrew Williams. The two men were Seneca's unofficial town fathers. "Mr. Williams or I will keep you informed. For now, keep a top eye open. Danger could be anywhere." The sermon was over. People stood and gathered their things.

Sooncy, who patterned much of her classroom style on the Reverend's own, was surprised he ended his sermon that way. For as long as she could remember, he had ended by saying "God smiles on Seneca Village. We are the lantern in the window of his house."

Far nicer words to start the week than "Danger could be anywhere."

8

THE ELLERTON HOME

THE FOLLOWING MONDAY, KAYLA TOLD Robert James Ellerton about her time with Sooncy. She started with the fun part early in the day. He was an eager listener. As an only child with no friends his own age, RJ looked forward to his time with pretty, kindhearted Kayla. It wasn't just that she always remembered to bring him a soothing drink to quench his thirst, or a small dish of food to ease his hunger. Her gentle presence alone seemed to calm him and subdue his illness.

Kayla's story fascinated him. The Ryan drinking house and Reinhold slaughterhouse weren't that far from his Eighty-seventh-Street home. Indeed Kayla's home was barely a fifteen-minute walk away. Yet they were all miles from his world. Kayla had never before spoken of her life in Seneca Village.

Her descriptions of the village were not at all what he had been led to believe by the newspapers, or his mother.

Kayla had, in fact, never spoken this much to him before at all. As she spoke, she saw herself as she never had before: as an interesting person with stories to tell. *My father would be proud*, she thought. Kayla looked directly into RJ's clear eyes instead of down as she usually did.

But when she came to the part about the men by the river who were sent by Mr. Villum, his eyes clouded over. A flush of anger colored his cheeks. "You're lucky to be alive, Kayla. I don't mean to alarm you any more than necessary, but they may hold true to their threat of crossing your path again." He shifted. Kayla helped him prop up his pillow. "Now we both know to take whatever my mother says with a grain of salt," he said with a slight smile, "but she has long suspected that your village, what with its sizable colored population, is a hiding place for runaway slaves. What do you think? Is it?"

Kayla thought for a moment. She wondered about the extra sacks of food and the unfamiliar laundry that tended to coincide with the appearance of people she didn't know. She shrugged.

"Kayla, the world is a dangerous place, and becoming more so all the time. Do you know about the Fugitive Slave Law?"

She shook her head. "Robert, you're not looking well. I think this is upsetting you. Let me get you some more tea, and then you should rest."

He smiled at her. "Sweet Kayla." She blushed. "It's important that you know this." Quickly and simply, he described the Underground Railroad, and how it was made up of abolitionists who sheltered runaway slaves. Then he explained the Fugitive Slave Law, stressing that anyone involved in hiding runaways was breaking the law and courting danger.

He put his hand on hers, making her heart race a bit. This was the most serious topic they had ever discussed. It was also the first time they had touched this way. She tried to focus on his words. She knew that what he was saying was important. "What you did was very brave, Kayla, but please, never do anything like that again. Stay away from the river—I'll tell Mother to let you have all the coals you want."

"No! She'll want to know why. And I don't want word of this getting back to my mother."

"I know. Don't worry. I'll take care of her. Just make sure you take care of yourself. You don't know what you're up against. This Mr. Villum must have plenty of money if he's paying for these slave catchers to travel north. When rich and powerful people want something, it's almost impossible to stop them."

He looked at Kayla. The girl had taken such good, tender care of him. She worked hard in his mother's house. Her burden of chores included the laundry and cooking as well as cleaning and serving. She hadn't been able to learn things of her new country beyond what his demanding mother had insisted on. He felt an immediate, crushing responsibility to take care of her. Just then, a new fear crossed his racing mind. "And Kayla, let no one into your house!"

She gasped. It was as though RJ knew of the horrible dream she'd had the last two nights, one in which the two men peered in her window, then knocked slowly and menacingly at the door. The only shred of mercy was that the dream ended before they entered.

RJ took both her hands in his. His palms were hot. "I've worried you and overworked myself. I admire what you did, Kayla, really. But Father says this whole country is like a tinderbox waiting to go up: Black against white. Democrats against Republicans. Slaveholders against abolitionists. North against South. So Kayla, avoid the fray—don't walk into it."

Suddenly, the duty of housework pushed aside the worries of a nation. "Your father! Today is his important meeting." She had overheard Mr. Ellerton making preparations for this meeting. He was a well-respected businessman and was hosting an important meeting that morning. The city's most influential politicians, businessmen, and city planners would all be there. Mrs. McBean had reminded the girl several times not to dawdle in RJ's room and to attend to Mr. Ellerton's needs promptly.

ONCE IN THE STUDY, KAYLA'S troubled mind went back to what RJ had told her. She barely noticed the discussion of the cigar-smoking men, their words wafting in and out of her awareness. Somehow, though, phrases such as "a much needed park" and "the welcome riddance of shantytowns" hung and unwound in her mind, much like their thick curls of tobacco smoke hung and unwound in the air.

9

SATURDAY, THE ROOT CELLAR

SOONCY HAD BEEN DOWN TO CALL ON MRS. Ryan to see if there were any messages to deliver that day. What she saw instead through Mrs. Ryan's barely opened door were the two slave catchers. They were passed out cold on her floor. Overhearing enough of their plans the night before to frighten her, Mrs. Ryan had slipped something extra in their drinks to prolong their sleep. She hoped Sooncy would show up before the drug wore off so she could warn her.

It just so happened that also the night before, more running-aways had come into the village. Sarah and her father, who planned to continue their trek northward that night, needed to be hidden elsewhere for the day.

Mrs. Taylor, recalling the McBean potato cellar

from years before, asked her daughter whether or not she thought Kayla would help. Sooncy answered that she knew she would.

As Sooncy headed down her stairs, a thought occurred to her. Only she knew the extent of the danger in which Kayla might find herself. She stopped and ran back up, and threw some boys' clothing into a sack.

If it worked for the running-aways, it would work for Kayla.

KAYLA ALREADY HAD ALL OF the wash hanging on the line. Officer Hale's thin bed sheets were nearly dry. She looked at his pile of mending and decided it could wait until after she'd had some lunch. She'd spent the past week in fear of seeing the slave catchers again—and had barely eaten at all.

Kayla thought of her father. She thought of Ireland, and ached for her earlier youth. She saw their thatched hut, a wee brown bump on a hill. She saw herself rolling down the hill with her cousins, like potatoes tumbling out of a sack. And she saw her strong, handsome father, tossing her up in the air, or gently cupping her face with his callused hand as she lay down in bed. She missed the tales he spun of Celtic warriors from whom the McBeans had descended—great big men who could put a leprechaun-sized girl like her in the palm of one hand. Kayla knew, though, that aside from these stolen moments of pleasure, Ireland had not been a happy place. But at least they had all been together. And at least the burden of unhappiness was in the ground with the failing crops, not on her shoulders.

She went inside to get some flour from the barrel in the cellar. As she scooped the flour, she heard a knock. She stopped and looked up. It happened again. Another knock. Immediately she thought of the two men. She froze momentarily, then slowly closed the barrel. Standing on the barrel, Kayla climbed out of the cellar. She peered out the kitchen window. Thank goodness for windows! It was Sooncy. Kayla was surprised. After last week, she never expected to talk to her again. With Sooncy was the girl Kayla had seen several nights ago, the girl who walked with a limp. Kayla opened the door. Quickly, the two came inside. Kayla noticed that the girl's limp was gone.

"I don't have much time. You've got to hide Sarah." Sooncy said.

"What?"

"You want to help, right? Hide her." Sooncy fumbled around in her bag, pulling out trousers, a button-down shirt, and a boy's jacket. She handed them to Kayla. "Here. Put these on." Kayla looked at her blankly, then at Sarah, who was clutching a tattered quilt.

"I don't understand," she said. But that was only half true. She didn't understand what the clothes were for yet, but she knew exactly why Sooncy had brought Sarah. She was a runaway slave, and Sooncy wanted Kayla to hide her. Exactly what RJ had said not to do.

"Please, Kayla. You've got to disguise yourself. Unless you want to hide as well, you've got to do this. We don't have much time. I have to rush back home and disguise myself, too. Those two men know we're here." As Sooncy described her trip to Mrs. Ryan's, Kayla took off her own clothes and put on the ones from Sooncy.

"When I left they were still as stone, but that won't last forever. When I ran home to tell my mother, she was helping out some new *arrivals*—running-aways we didn't expect for a few days. Mama said we had to listen to the Reverend's words and seek out assistance from those we might not ordinarily go to. We're asking for your help now, Kayla. Mama remembered your root cellar from when she was here years ago. She asked me if I thought you'd help. I told her that I knew you would."

Kayla listened both to what Sooncy said, and to what she didn't. She couldn't believe Mrs. Taylor would suggest coming to this house if she'd known Kayla was at the river, too. It would be too risky. "You didn't tell your mother all that happened last week, did you?"

Sooncy stood still. The shelf clock that Mrs. Ellerton had given the McBeans to insure that they were prompt ticked loudly. Sooncy shook her head.

Kayla nodded. "I didn't tell mine, either."

Sooncy looked at Kayla, wishing then that the two had become friends sooner. They were a good pair, each a complement to the other. She looked forward to spending time with this quiet girl. Now, however, was not the time to worry about missed opportunities of the past. It was, instead, time to prepare for the worrisome future.

Sooncy reached into the sack. "Here." She handed Kayla a porkpie hat. "Just stuff your hair in there. Take off your boots too, girlie. Go barefoot." She looked out the window, then back at Kayla, who was tucking her wisps of hair out of sight. "Good. Once you get those boots off you'll look like one of the boys." She managed a smile.

"Now. Sarah." Sooncy's eyes went to the open root cellar. "There." Sarah looked at Sooncy, then at Kayla. Slowly, Kayla nodded. RJ had warned her of the smart thing to do. This, though, seemed the right thing to do.

"It's just for the day, Sarah," Sooncy said to the girl.

Sarah moved toward the cellar, then stopped to speak to Kayla. "I have to thank you now, because I don't know what the rest of the day will bring. I just pray the Lord delivers us all safely into the Sabbath." As she climbed down she added, "And we all thought once we came to New York we'd be home free. Guess being free doesn't mean being safe."

Before the door closed, Sooncy added, "Remember Sarah, no matter what you may hear, stay put."

"Believe me, I know," Sarah responded. "This ain't the first cellar I've holed up in." She gathered the quilt about her and closed the door.

No one noticed the small bit of fabric caught in the hinge.

Kayla followed Sooncy outside. She felt odd in her disguise. She wanted to stay inside, but didn't want to hear the girl moving or even breathing down there.

She took Sooncy's arm. "What about you? You need a disguise, too."

"I had to get you two settled first. I'm running back home right now." She squeezed Kayla's hand and turned to go.

"Wait! When will you come for her?"

"Tonight, at dusk. She and her Pa are leaving tonight. Tell no one. Take care. And thank you, friend." She turned and quickly walked away.

Kayla's deep pleasure at Sooncy's parting words was rapidly replaced by terror. Those horrible men were nearby. What would they do if they found her?

She felt danger twist her stomach like wet laundry. She looked down at her bare feet. *How odd I must look. And, I hope, how unlike myself.* She looked at the pile of mending. *I'll look ridiculous doing mending out here now. Boys never sew. Not unless they're making a ball out of pigskin. Besides, if this getup is successful, the neighbors will get suspicious seeing some strange boy in our yard.*

As she paced back and forth, her racing mind leaped to another possible calamity—her mother! What if she found out what was going on in her very own home? But, no, she wouldn't. She was hard at work at the Ellertons. She wouldn't be home until nine o'clock that night. *Calm yourself. No one's about. Just wait. Night will come. The girl will go.*

MRS. MCBEAN HEADED FOR HOME. It felt peculiar to walk home in broad daylight. But none other than Mrs. Ellerton had instructed her to do so. Both women knew that RJ found more comfort in Mrs. McBean's Irish cures than any of the potions prescribed by the fancy doctors that paraded past his bed. His health had been too shaky for too long. It was time to have Mrs. McBean's folk medicine take over where modern medicine was lacking.

There was just a bit of herb left in the cellar.

10

CONFRONTATION

KAYLA STAYED IN THE YARD, DISTRACTEDLY mending. Despite her earlier decision not to sew, pacing about aimlessly had made her heart beat so fast she feared it would stop. So lost in her thoughts and fears, she was barely aware of the several needle pricks where she'd missed the worn sock and jabbed herself instead.

Sheila McBean walked south along Spring Street. Her thoughts of RJ were interrupted by what she saw in her side yard. *Who is that boy leaning against my house? Odd how he has my Kayla's frame. Same chin, too. And what's he doing sewing?* Several more paces and she realized who it was.

"What on earth is going on here? Is this what you do on your day off, dress as a boy?"

Kayla looked up in horror. She hadn't heard her

mother's approach. "Mother. Please. Don't raise your voice so. I can explain."

"Get in the house this instant. And take that hat off," she said angrily, yanking it off Kayla's head. Kayla's dark brown curls tumbled down her back. She pushed inside ahead of her mother, knocking Mrs. McBean roughly into the doorjamb.

"Kayla! What's come over you?"

Just then, both noticed the quilt. Slowly, Mrs. McBean walked over to the trap door, picked up the lid, and peered inside. Sarah's small face looked up solemnly.

"Mother of God! Kayla! What in the name of sweet Mary is going on here?"

Quickly and concisely, Kayla described for her mother as well as she could the morning's events.

"I'm scared mother. But we can't turn this girl out. We can't."

Just then, there was a knock at the door. Her heart in her throat, Kayla closed the cellar again. She tried jamming the quilt back in, but it was stuck in the hinge. Mrs. McBean went to the door.

It was Officer Hale, still in uniform. Never had Mrs. McBean been so pleased to see him. But what, if anything, should she tell him? She knew he fancied her, but what would he think of her harboring a runaway slave? Good Lord, she was harboring a fugitive. Her mind snapped back to attention.

Would he protect her, or turn her in?

"Good afternoon, Sheila. I heard a little ruckus here. Is there a problem?"

"Problem? No. Just a mother-daughter squabble."

Mr. Hale peered in at Kayla. Dressed as she was she appeared more like a young hoodlum down in New York City than a young lady. He scratched his head, certain that if he lived to be a hundred years old, he would never understand women.

"Well anyhow, I just thought I'd come by and pick up my laundry. Maybe have some tea with you two . . . ladies." He paused, looking confusedly at Kayla again. He stood in the doorway uneasily, hands fidgeting with the day stick that hung from his belt. He'd rarely been invited in, and it looked as though today would be no exception.

Kayla could hear Sarah's heartbeat surer than her own. She was certain Mr. Hale would hear it, too. "Oh my—your wash! I forgot. Let me get it down." Small as she was, she nearly knocked him down as she ran past. Although frightened to be outside not fully disguised, the more immediate fear of having Mr. Hale too close to Sarah was more than she could bear. She, too, had no idea how he felt about harboring fugitive slaves. The duty of a decent human? Or a criminal act to be punished?

The adults followed Kayla to the clothesline. She began taking down the sun-crisped clothes. Then she noticed two figures in the distance. As they came closer, she could see they walked a bit unsteadily. Squinting against the sun, she recognized their frayed silhouettes.

The thin one noticed Kayla first, nudging his partner. They smiled menacingly, walking straight for her. Her heart nearly stopped in panic, but her hands kept working furiously. As her mother made nervous small talk with her caller, a thought occurred to Kayla. The two men hadn't yet seen Officer Hale. Tall and fit as he was, he remained hidden by the bed sheet. Quickly, without undoing the clothespins, Kayla ripped the sheet off the line. The ferocity of the movement startled everyone, and tore the sheet. But it accomplished her aim— revealing the imposing figure of an officer of the law, suited up from head to toe, in her yard.

A father, home from work.

Officer Hale looked with worried confusion at Kayla. What was wrong with this girl today? Following her anguished gaze, he looked past the laundry at the two disreputable looking men heading their way. A good stone's throw away, they stopped a moment, then resumed walking.

Partly as a show of bravado for Mrs. McBean, and partly as the good officer and neighbor he was, Officer Hale asked loudly what business the two had in these parts.

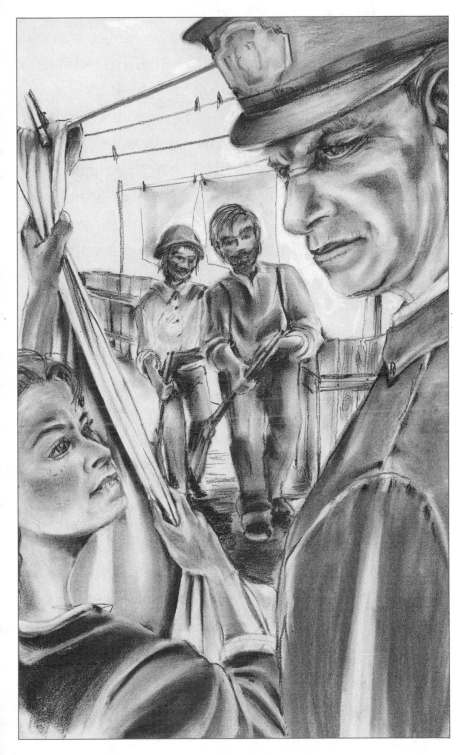

"We have no drinking establishments here," he said, sniffing disapprovingly at their boozy stench as they came closer. With a flourish he twirled his stick, and advised them quite sternly to be on their way.

Willard was unfazed. "We're not after drink. We're after lost property—three runaway slaves we mean to return to their rightful owner. We have reason to believe they're hidden here. I wouldn't be surprised if they were on these very premises." He nodded at the McBean house. Kayla was confused. *Three* runaways? She only knew of two. Did they mean to take Sooncy? But she wasn't a slave!

With all the sincerity of one who believes what he's saying to be the gospel truth, Mr. Hale told them there was no such activity going on in this village. And, he told them, unless they wanted to be shipped off to jail—after getting a taste of his locust stick—they'd best leave the premises immediately.

But the two held their ground. Edmund poked a dirty finger in Kayla's direction. "Where's your little darkie friend?"

"Now, now," Mr. Hale interrupted angrily. He'd been leading prayer groups in his home for coloreds and whites for years. No one came into his town and spoke this way. "We'll not have talk like that, here. This is a decent community where we treat each other with respect. If you can't tolerate the thought of colored and white folks living together in peace, then get back to your plantation or whatever god-forsaken wasteland you come from."

"Not before we have some water," Willard said. "That spring we passed ain't private property."

The two snorted, skulking off like angry, thwarted children. Muttering about uncivilized Northerners, they said that the stinking Irish and blacks could have each other and go to the devil.

The McBeans and Mr. Hale stood in the silence that followed. Mrs. McBean was quite still. She was ashamed of what she, herself, had felt about having colored neighbors. Quietly, she expressed her gratitude to Mr. Hale for what he had done, and what he had said. Kayla gathered up his laundry.

Mrs. McBean turned to her daughter. "Kayla, you can't stay here now. Come back with me to the Ellertons. And on the way you can explain your behavior and how those men seemed to recognize you."

Kayla understood that she owed her mother an explanation. What's more, although she knew that RJ was in good hands, she was still concerned about him. It was just that she, herself, had someone to look after. RJ needed her mother, but Sarah needed her.

None of this, though, could she explain in front of Officer Hale. How she wished that her father were there. Not realizing what she was doing, she cupped her own face, just as he had done so many times. When she looked up at her mother, she recognized that a change had come over her, softening her features.

Mrs. McBean nodded at Kayla, then looked past her daughter toward the rocky landscape. How was it she had never noticed how much it looked like home? Then, deep inside, she heard the rich, Irish voice she knew so well. *That's a lovely daughter by your side, Sheila McBean. Wise and kind-hearted. Trust her.*

Mrs. McBean looked at Kayla and nodded again. A quiet "Aye" escaped her lips.

Silently, Kayla thanked both her parents.

Officer Hale cleared his throat.

Mrs. McBean cleared her head and turned to him. As she quickly explained the situation at the Ellertons, Kayla went into the house. She reached down to get the small pouch of herbs, whispering to Sarah that the danger had passed, but that it was most likely best to stay below until nightfall, just in case. She deftly yanked the quilt without tearing it, placing the telltale corner in Sarah's hand.

Kayla handed the herbs to her mother. Mrs. McBean looked into her daughter's eyes for a long moment. Kayla had expected a torrent of anger for putting them in such danger. Although pleased she was being allowed to stay, she felt uncomfortable in the silence.

Mrs. McBean reached for Officer Hale's hand. "Please keep her with you today. She's all I have."

His cheeks reddened as he nodded. Mrs. McBean brushed a tear from her cheek, crossed herself, and turned back for Bloomingdale.

Mr. Hale, looking at the disappearing figure of Mrs. McBean, said aloud, "Come Kayla. We're going on patrol."

Before Kayla could protest, he had taken several long strides toward Spring Street. She had to run to catch up.

11

THE REAL POT OF GOLD

MR. GABLE WAS WHITTLING IN HIS BACKYARD when Willard and Edmund showed up. He was the real "pot of gold"—a fugitive slave who had run away five years earlier. His former master, a vindictive man bent on revenge, had been determined to capture him ever since.

"I've been waiting on you people. Took you long enough."

"Glad to see you're being sensible," Willard said, relieved to see the man wasn't going to put up a fight. He did wish he weren't holding a knife, though. "Why don't you go into the house and get your stuff together. Not much," he added. "We don't have the room."

Mr. Gable nodded, but made no move to get up.

Willard and Edmund looked at one another.

Edmund stuck his pointy chin at Mr. Gable. "Don't start wasting our time now. You should've run North like the rest of 'em when you had the chance. Not stay here all these years."

"I chose not to."

Willard laughed. "You *chose*? Tell me about it, old man." Having his quarry in his sites and the law on his side, he didn't mind extending the moment of victory. He put his hands on his hips and spat out a wad of tobacco. He was ready for a story. Edmund crossed his arms.

Mr. Gable, who had dreamed of this meeting for years, readily obliged.

Slowly and deliberately, like one who had waited a lifetime to speak, he told his tale. "I came north by boat, smuggled aboard by a black sailor. He brought me here to his home to rest up first. His wife looked after me and fed me. She tended to my wounds from that horrible trip, and the horrible life before it. When I was up and able, I looked around. What I saw was a most miraculous place, and I don't hold with miracles. Keep running north? How could I leave a place like this? A town of free colored people. Owned their own property. Owned themselves. Heck, men here could even vote. Women owned land! Colored women! And white folks living here—side by side with colored folks. Because they chose to. Weren't no slum, neither. Pretty little place." He put his hand into his pocket. The two Southerners immediately went for their guns, then paused when they saw him pull out a shiny gold coin. "Look at that. My own half-eagle. I earned that five dollars. Earned it right here in New York. And it's gonna stay in New York." He put it back into his pocket. "This is the only part of my life that's mattered." He unbuttoned the top of his shirt, showing the welts across his chest matching the one across his cheek. "You think where you come from was part of a life worth living? Seneca Village is going to have to leave before I leave it. I am not going back to the Villum plantation. You'll have to kill me first. How much you think Villum'll give you for my dead body?"

Willard crossed his arms across his big chest. "Maybe we didn't make ourselves clear. You think Villum—and that's Master Villum to you—wants you back alive? He don't care. Prefers you alive, but he'll take you whichever way he can. He's gonna win either way. Those were his words. You're property. You ain't a man. I'll shoot you right now, throw you in a sack, and take you that way if I have to. It's up to you. That's your choice now. "

Edmund spoke up. He didn't relish the thought of dragging a heavy body downtown. "You might as well come. You'll probably get free in a few years. This whole country's fixing to blow. All those Yankee agitators—trying to run slavery into the ground—taking money outta a poor white man's pocket."

Willard was tired of this. "All right old man. Get moving. Either that or I shoot. I really don't care if you live or die." He started reaching for his gun.

A voice from behind the two men spoke up. "You should care. You'll die, too."

The slave catchers turned to see Officer Hale pointing a gun at them. As they looked around, they saw that they were surrounded. There was a group of twenty or so people: white and black, men and women. They appeared from behind sheds, outhouses, and stables. On a hunch, Mr. Hale had told Kayla to fetch a friend and round up all the folks from his prayer group. Everyone who was home came immediately. Just about everyone came armed. Kayla and Sooncy watched in fearful fascination.

At first startled, Willard smiled. "Now, Officer. I know you won't stop us from carrying out our legal responsibility. Maybe you missed it, but Mr. Gable has considerately identified himself as Mr. Villum's missing property." Willard moved so that he could see both the officer and Mr. Gable. "Besides, I know you won't kill us. You're an officer of the law." His precarious position did little to remove the insolence from his tone.

"True. I am," Mr. Hale said with equal mock sincerity. "And as an officer, I know it's awful tricky to

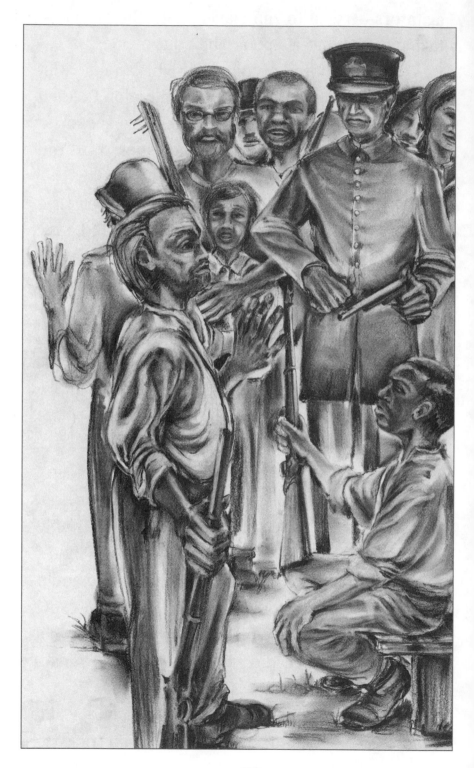

prove that a crime—say an accidental killing—has been committed without the proper evidence thereof."

Accidental killing? Willard and Edmund looked around uneasily. Everywhere they looked they saw weapons of one kind or another. Small guns, rifles, knives. One man had a board with nails sticking out of one end. And then there was Mr. Gable. He had put down his knife and taken his rifle out of its case.

A white man with a pistol spoke up. "How much you figure Moller would give for the bones?"

A tall black woman with a long kitchen knife responded. "I don't know, what do you think, Rose?"

The white woman next to her, whose clean knife glinted in the sun, considered this. "Personally, I'd go down to Menck's instead. He pays more for bones than anyone. Must boil 'em down to gold."

The villagers, all well-seasoned barterers, chuckled. Two pigs, as though anticipating a meal, sniffed at the men.

Officer Hale's next-door neighbor got closer. "And those pistols," he said, whistling. "They'd fetch a good price. I don't know about the clothes, though," he said, waving a hand in front of his nose. "Even old Bessie wouldn't want those." The villagers laughed, feeling their power grow. The two men seemed to shrink before them.

Officer Hale walked over to them. He took their guns, now limp in their hands. "We'll take these." He stuck them in his belt. "Now you go. Go back to Dixie." He paused. "Now," he said softly. The two men walked slowly, then ran toward the boulevard, nearly getting run down by a passing carriage.

For a good while, everyone stood around, asking questions and slapping each other on their backs. They quieted as Mr. Gable told his whole story.

Sooncy listened with astonishment as she heard that it was none other than her own father who had smuggled Mr. Gable into town. And it was her mother who had nursed him back to health. No one in the whole village, in fact, aside from her parents, had known that Mr. Gable was actually a fugitive slave.

"How come I never knew it was my own daddy who brought you?" Sooncy asked.

"Reckon he thought it might not be a secret anymore. Just knowing something ain't cause enough to say it. Not by a long shot."

Sooncy bit her lip and looked down.

As the talk continued, Officer Hale turned to Kayla. "Let's go back to your house. We have some unfinished business."

Kayla stared up at him.

"Let's get that poor soul out of your cellar."

They walked along through wandering dogs and neighbors' laundry. Kayla asked worriedly, "How did you know?"

He reached out and touched the corner of a quilt hanging on a line, tugging it slightly as he kept moving.

Sooncy ran to catch up with them.

THE TOWNSPEOPLE WERE RELIVING their success. Already they were adding embellishments that all there would forever swear to. As with all history, this episode, too, would be written by the victors. What they didn't know then, though, was that it was to be the last full page of Seneca Village history written by them.

The final page, the final chapter, would be written by outsiders. In disappearing ink.

12

A PLACE IN THE WORLD

WHEN THE SKY WENT FROM BLUE TO BLUSH the next morning, Kayla had already been up for several hours. Not cleaning or mending, just thinking of the night before.

At candle-lighting that night, when the first stars had appeared over the reservoir, someone knocked lightly on the door. It was Sarah. She had stopped by to say goodbye. "Here," she said to Kayla. "I want you to have this." She handed Kayla the quilt. Kayla held it admiringly. The multi-colored boxes looked like real stacked blocks, like if you shook the thing they would tumble off into a pile on the floor. It was soft, beautiful, and like no quilt she'd ever seen. But she handed it back. It was far too precious a gift.

Sarah wouldn't take it, though. She pointed at Kayla's small bed. "That where you sleep?" Kayla nodded. "I'll take that one in exchange." She lifted the hole-riddled, woolen blanket. "It'll keep me warm on those Canada nights I'm heading to."

Kayla protested. "But you can't. It's not an even trade by any means."

Gently, Sarah took the quilt from Kayla and laid it on her bed. She slung the woolen blanket over her shoulder and looked directly into Kayla's eyes. "It is."

AS KAYLA STUDIED THE QUILT'S intricate stitches Sunday morning, there was a soft tapping at the window. It startled Kayla out of her thoughts, but didn't wake her mother out of her sleep.

It was Sooncy. Kayla joined her outside. The warm June sun was just coming up, and the two girls sat on the cool slab of rock jutting from under the front door. In perfect silence, they watched as the sun rose over the tall stone reservoir, slowly illuminating the village. The sparkling white boards of All Angels' angled to face the sunrise. The wide gray boards of Grocer Pease's house, even the rough planks of Mr. White's outhouse looked promising in the golden light. The summer of fifty-five sat before them like a gift waiting to be opened.

Kayla thought about Sarah's patient victory and her quest for a new home. She smiled, grateful she had already found her place in the world. And a friend to share it with.

Seneca Village was torn down by the city in 1857. The last of the 1,600 inhabitants of the entire area that would become Central Park were removed that year. A clear plan of what it would look like was not agreed upon until a competition was held the following year. The winning entry, called the Greensward Plan, was submitted by Calvert Vaux and Frederick Law Olmstead. At approximately eight hundred acres, the creation of Central Park was seen as one of America's greatest physical undertakings of the nineteenth century.

For the most part, the landscape of the future park was bleak. The exception was Seneca Village. It sat between West Eighty-second and West Eighty-eighth Streets, just east of what was then Eighth Avenue, now Central Park West. There, modest but well-made homes were laid out in orderly fashion along unpaved streets. The main thoroughfare had three churches and a school. First settled in 1825 by African Americans, by 1855 it was a racially mixed community that included Irish and German immigrants and white native-born Americans.

Just as this community was expanding and diversifying, though, the call for a large park grew louder. The city was crowded and dirty. People needed a scenic rest from it all. It was agreed that the island's disagreeable midsection would be the best location. Residents could be paid to leave their homes and businesses. The land could then be cleared, drained, replanted, and beautified. Thus Central Park was born.

If you were to enter Central Park at its West Eighty-fifth Street entrance today, you'd have a hard time visualizing Seneca Village. The park's seemingly natural beauty was actually carefully designed and engineered, removing most traces of its former life. Few markers of pre-park life still exist. Nanny Goat Hill was renamed Summit Rock. Some large cobblestones inside the park along where Eighty-fifth Street would have continued are believed to be remnants of All Angels' foundation. Farther south, at Sixty-sixth Street, Tavern on the Green restaurant stands where William Menck's bone-boiling factory once did.

Research into Seneca Village's past is difficult. There are no known photos of the village. In fact, historians say, few personal records of the village or villagers exist at all. Public records reveal that the landowners of Seneca Village were compensated upon eviction. To date, no clear record exists of where they went. It is known that they did not form a new community together. Like a disassembled quilt, the individual squares, however beautiful, were never as much so as when sewn together.

It wasn't until the 1992 publication of *The Park and the People*, written by historians Roy Rosenzweig and

Elizabeth Blackmar, that the existence of Seneca Village became widely known. That book, which details all of Central Park's history, inspired the creation of an exhibit and Web site by the New-York Historical Society: www.nyhistory.org. Written and run by historians Grady Turner and Cynthia Copeland, this site focuses on Seneca Village.

Seneca Village as a possible stop on the Underground Railroad, or as a permanent residence for fugitive slaves, is a fictionalized account of what might have happened. No records have yet been uncovered to prove whether or not townspeople played any role in helping fugitive slaves escape would-be captors. Although Andrew Williams and Reverend Leven Smith were important fixtures in Seneca Village, their actions in this story are fictionalized. Officer Hale is based on another real person, Officer Evers, who with his wife did hold prayer-group meetings for blacks and whites in his home.

Information about the use of quilts in the time of slavery can be found in *Hidden in Plain View*, by Jaqueline L. Tobin and Raymond G. Dobard.

1821 A New York State law is passed barring African-American men from voting unless they own $250 worth of property.

1825 Cartman John Whitehead and his wife, Elizabeth, begin selling off parcels of their Upper West Side farmland in what was to become Seneca Village. Andrew Williams, then a bootblack, later a cartman, buys the first three lots. Cost: $125

1827 Slavery in New York State is abolished.

1838 New York displaces the residents of York Hill by buying that land and putting the receiving basin for the Croton Reservoir there.

1840 More than one hundred people, mostly African Americans, live in Seneca Village.

1851 Peak year for Irish immigration to the United States.

1853 The city legislature passes a bill authorizing that roughly eight hundred acres in the middle of Manhattan Island will be taken over by eminent domain to create a public park. Landowners will be paid after their property is valued by city surveyors. The process of putting dollar figures on the 7,500 lots of land will take over two years.

1855 The New York State census shows Seneca Village as home to over 260 people. Irish Americans make up about 30 percent of the community, but German immigrants and native-born whites live there as well. This will be the last year the census is taken in Seneca Village; the community will be erased from the landscape within two years. The city compensates petitioning landowners. Andrew Williams receives $2,335 for his three lots and two-story frame house.

1856 Park-area residents and landowners are ordered to vacate by August.

1857 All trace of the 1,600 residents of what will be Central Park is cleared away.

READING LIST/SELECTED SOURCES

Until publication of *Upper West Side Story* (Abbeville Press, Inc., 1989) by Peter Salwen, and most notably *The Park and the People: A History of Central Park* (Ithaca and London: Cornell University Press, 1992) by Roy Rosenzweig and Elizabeth Blackmar, very little had been written about Seneca Village. Inspired by *The Park and the People,* a scholarly book intended for adults, The New-York Historical Society (NYHS) created a museum exhibit and subsequent Web site at www.nyhistory.org. Targeted for children, the NYHS's offerings were devoted fully to exploring the true nature of life in the then maligned, now largely forgotten village. Both *The Park and the People* and the New-York Historical Society Web site were the primary information sources for *The Lost Village of Central Park.*

Many thanks to Cynthia R. Copeland and Grady Turner of the New-York Historical Society for allowing the following information to be printed here. The text is largely theirs, with a few references from this book added.

Enter Central Park at West Eighty-fifth Street, called Mariners' Gate. Imagine that Eighty-fifth Street continues straight into the park and try to follow its path. You'll see a playground beyond the benches to your right. At the ginkgo tree, cross the road and walk up the hill. Spector Playground is on your left. Follow the imaginary Eighty-fifth Street downhill, walking past the granite mound on your right. Cross the West Drive and walk through the pines.

Pass the swing set and walk toward the Great Lawn. Stop at the path. Look back over the route you have traveled. Now try to imagine how your walk would have looked before Central Park, if you were Mr. Williams taking his horse and cart home, or Kayla coming home from work. Remember—Seneca Village received no city services such as gaslights.

The landscape then was entirely different. The oldest trees visible today had not yet been planted. The boundaries of west Eighty-fifth Street actually did continue to the spot where you are standing, where it ended at the great wall of the reservoir, which covered the current site of the Great Lawn.

Retrace your steps. As you walk west, near West

Drive, on your right were Andrew Williams's property, the AME Zion Church next door, and a cemetery with a greenhouse beyond. (Mr. Williams's house sat on the adjacent lot to the north, its entrance on Eighty-sixth Street.)

Across the street, on the south side of Eighty-fifth Street, stood the African Union Methodist Church. If school were in session, you might hear Sooncy or Catherine Thompson, Seneca Village's schoolteacher, leading a class in recitations.

Cross Old Lane (also referred to as Spring Street—the spring is still just a few blocks south) to reach All Angels' Church. Off the path and on the grass to the left are some foundation stones. Historians believe they were those of the church.

As you walk downhill, you'll pass through the church cemetery (presumably still there). Stop at the gate. Look back. A village of nearly three hundred people once stood on this land. Between 1825 and 1856, Seneca Village became New York State's first substantial community of African-American landowners. During that same thirty-year period, New York City's population almost quadrupled—from 165,000 to 630,000. By 1855 nearly half of the people living in Manhattan had been born in another country, most often Ireland or Germany. As some of those immigrants found their way to Seneca Village, it became a model of an integrated neighborhood.